WITHDRAWAL

GOOD KING WENCESLAS

BY JOHN MASON NEALE, WITH ILLUSTRATIONS & ORNAMENTS BY CHRISTOPHER MANSON

NORTH·SOUTH BOOKS

All **G**ood King **W**enceslas look'd out, On the feast of Stephen, **W**hen the snow lay round about, Deep and crisp and even;

All **B**rightly shone the moon that night, Tho' the frost was cruel, **W**hen a poor man came in sight, Gath'ring winter fuel.

King Hither, page, and stand by me, If thou know'st it, telling; Yonder peasant, who is he? Where and what his dwelling?

Page **S**ire, he lives a good league ⊘ hence, Underneath the mountain; **R**ight ⊘ ⊘ against the forest fence, By St. Agnes' fountain.

King **B**ring me flesh and bring me ❧ wine, Bring me pine logs hither; **T**hou and I ❧ ❧ will see him ❧ dine When we bear them thither.

All **P**age and monarch forth they went, forth they went together; **T**hro' the rude wind's wild  lament And the bitter weather.

Page Sire, the night
is darker now,
And the wind
blows stronger;
Fails my heart,
I know not
how, I can go
no longer.

King **Mark my footsteps, my good page, Tread thou in them boldly; Thou shalt find the winter's rage freeze thy blood less coldly.**

All In his master's steps he trod, Where the snow lay dinted; Heat was in the very sod Which the saint had printed.

All Therefore, Christian men, be sure, Wealth or rank possessing, Ye who now will bless the poor, Shall yourselves find blessing.

Good King Wen ⁄ ces ⁄ las look'd out

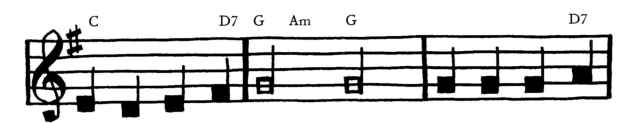

On the Feast of Ste ⁄ phen, When the snow lay

round a ⁄ bout, Deep and crisp and e ⁄ ven.

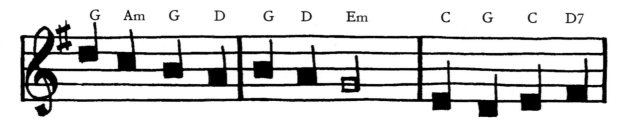

Bright-ly shone the moon that night, Though the frost was

cru — el, When a poor man came in sight,

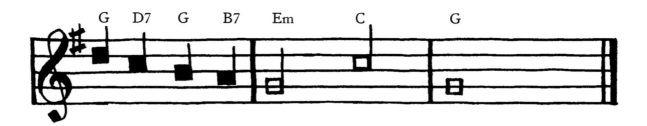

Gath-'ring win-ter fu — el.

 ENCESLAS, Duke of Bohemia, was raised by his grandmother as a Christian in a land that, in the early tenth century, was still largely pagan. At about twenty years of age, Wenceslas took over leadership of Bohemia from his mother, who was a harsh and unpopular ruler. He encouraged the spread of Christianity and public order; there were many popular stories recounting his concern for his people and his generosity to the poor. In 929 he made a treaty with the powerful German King Henry I, who was also a Christian; in exchange for peace, Wenceslas agreed to pay tribute to his neighbor and allow German priests to do missionary work in Bohemia. A faction of pagan nobles, led by the duke's younger brother, Boleslav, opposed the treaty and plotted against him. On the way to Mass, Wenceslas was attacked by his brother and the nobles, and was slain at the gates of the church. He became the patron saint of the Bohemian, or Czech, people. His statue presides over the main public square in Prague—Wenceslas Square.

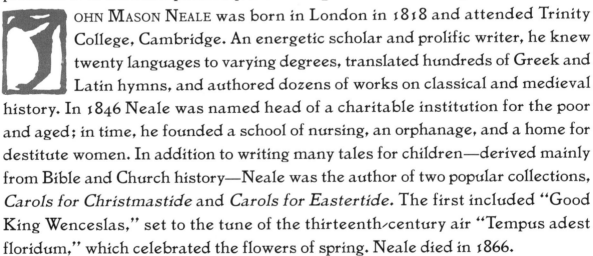 OHN MASON NEALE was born in London in 1818 and attended Trinity College, Cambridge. An energetic scholar and prolific writer, he knew twenty languages to varying degrees, translated hundreds of Greek and Latin hymns, and authored dozens of works on classical and medieval history. In 1846 Neale was named head of a charitable institution for the poor and aged; in time, he founded a school of nursing, an orphanage, and a home for destitute women. In addition to writing many tales for children—derived mainly from Bible and Church history—Neale was the author of two popular collections, *Carols for Christmastide* and *Carols for Eastertide*. The first included "Good King Wenceslas," set to the tune of the thirteenth-century air "Tempus adest floridum," which celebrated the flowers of spring. Neale died in 1866.

Published in the United States by North-South Books Inc., New York. Published simultaneously in Great Britain, Canada, Australia, and New Zealand in 1994 by North-South Books, an imprint of Nord-Süd Verlag AG, Gossau Zürich, Switzerland.

Library of Congress Cataloging-in-Publication Data. Neale, J.M. (John Mason), 1818-1866. Good King Wenceslas / by John Mason Neale ; with illustrations and ornaments by Christopher Manson. Summary: Illustrated text of the well-known carol is accompanied by a brief history of the real Wenceslas, Duke of Bohemia. 1. Carols, English—Texts. 2. Wenceslas, Duke of Bohemia, ca. 907-929—Juvenile literature. [1. Carols. 2. Christmas music. 3. Wenceslas, Duke of Bohemia, ca. 907-929.] I. Manson, Christopher, ill. II. Title. PZ8.3.N315Go 1994 782.42'1723'00268—dc20 94-17443

A CIP catalogue record for this book is available from The British Library. The illustrations are woodcuts, painted with watercolor. The text was hand lettered and cut in wood by the artist. Musical arrangement by Frank Metis.

ISBN 1-55858-321-1 (TRADE BINDING)
ISBN 1-55858-322-X (LIBRARY BINDING)
1 3 5 7 9 TB 10 8 6 4 2
1 3 5 7 9 LB 10 8 6 4 2
Printed in Belgium